Zippy

and the

Stripes of Courage

Zippy

and the

Stripes of Courage

Written by Candida Sullivan

Illustrated by Jack Foster

Special note from Dr. Rick Metrick

Copyright @ 2011 ShadeTree Publishing, LLC

1038 N. Eisenhower Dr. #274

Beckley, West Virginia 25801

ISBN: 978-1-937331-08-5

Printed in the United States of America

Visit our Web site at www.ShadeTreePublishing.com

To Cayden, Jordon, and Avery. Thank you for brightening my life. C.S.

To my grandson Johnny, with love and hope for great things in your future. J.F.

A story about a zebra named Zippy who didn't look like the others...

Zippy ducked into the shadows and watched the animals play. He wanted to play, too, but was afraid to ask. Besides, exactly whom was he supposed to play with anyway? He was the only zebra without black stripes in all of Grassy Plains.

"Am I still a zebra if I don't have stripes?" Zippy wondered.

He hated it when the other animals teased him about his stripes or rather the lack of them. He hated when they stared at him. It made him feel ashamed.

He stammered to the stream and lowered his head.
A tear dripped and rippled the water.

When the water cleared, Zippy saw a ghost staring back at him. "Yikes!" he screamed and stumbled backwards.

He knew he should run away, but instead he peeped into the water—with one eye open. The ghost stared back.

He blinked once, then twice. The ghost remained.

He wiggled his ears. The ghost mimicked him.

Zippy smiled and the ghost smiled.

Then, Zippy giggled as he realized there was no such thing as ghosts. It was only his reflection.

A noise startled Zippy and he turned to see a group of zebras staring at him. He started to run away, but he remembered what his mom had told him about making friends.

"Just be you and they'll love you," he could hear her saying.

"Hi! I'm Zippy," he said, as he stood tall.

"Please don't hurt us!" they stuttered.

"I won't hurt you, but I would like to play," Zippy admitted.

"Can ghosts play?" they asked.

"I'm not a ghost," Zippy said. "I'm a zebra, without stripes."

"Why don't you have stripes?" Golly, the lead male zebra asked. "Did they fall off? Are you sure you're really a zebra? Will our stripes disappear if we play with you?"

Zippy got so tired of the same questions. That's why he usually hid, so no one would stare or ask him about his stripes.

"I was born without them," Zippy explained. "My mom and dad have stripes. Everyone in my family has stripes except me."

Golly looked relieved and invited Zippy to play.

For a moment, Zippy forgot that he didn't have stripes. He felt normal as he raced around the plains with his new friends.

And then, everything changed...

The zebras decided to venture over to Forbidden Ridge to play. So, they all lined up at Crocodile Crossing, according to the width of their stripes.

Since Golly's stripes were the widest, he was deemed the bravest and elected to go first. Everyone crossed the stream – everyone except for Zippy that is.

He froze at the edge and his legs trembled.

Zippy stood near the crossing alone.

"Come on, Zippy," they beckoned.

Zippy closed his eyes and lowered his head.

"What's wrong, Zippy? Are you afraid?" Golly asked.

Zippy started to open his mouth to deny it, but he knew that it was really true. He felt his tears well up and sting his eyes.

"Zippy, the cowardly ghost," the other zebras chanted.

"I hate stripes!" he yelled. "Who wants a bunch of big stripes anyway?" Turning to leave, he whispered, "I do, God." He wondered what he had done to make God mad at him. Why didn't God give him stripes like everyone else? Why was he different? Zippy dropped his head and dawdled away.

Suddenly, Zippy stopped because he heard the other zebras coming back. He looked over his shoulder and saw hyenas chasing the zebras. "Help us, Zippy!" they pleaded.

With his feelings still hurt, Zippy decided to hurry away.

"Where are you going, Zippy? Aren't you going to help your friends?" asked Naomi the wise owl.

"Why should I help them? They're not my friends. They laughed and called me names."

"Now Zippy," Naomi gently instructed. "You know that we are supposed to treat others *how we want to be treated*, not *how they've treated us*."

Zippy's lip quivered. "But, I'm a-f-f-fraid."

"It's okay to be frightened, Zippy. True bravery is doing the right thing even when you're scared."

"Really?" Zippy asked.

Naomi nodded and patted Zippy on the head. Before she had a chance to say anything else, Zippy rushed away.

Trapped between the hyenas and the gathering crocodiles, the other zebras were crying and begging for help.

Zippy quickly devised a plan to save them. Pretending to be a ghost, he stood on his back legs and walked like a zombie. He moaned and groaned as loud as he could. As he stumbled toward the hyenas, they began to run for their lives.

Zippy successfully outsmarted the hyenas. However, there was still another danger at hand – the crocodiles.

He decided to be brave once more and marched right over to the edge of the crossing.

"Mr. Crocodile, will you please allow my friends to cross your stream?" Zippy asked the largest crocodile there.

"Hmmm," he said. "Why are you trying to help them, Zippy? They teased you."

"I know," Zippy said. "But we're supposed to help those in need. That's what a real friend does. Being mean to them will only hurt their feelings, just like it did mine."

The crocodile sighed. He liked Zippy. He had never met a zebra so brave.

"Your friends may cross the stream," he said to Zippy. Then he turned to the other zebras. "Zippy was brave, today. He is the bravest zebra I have ever seen."

All the zebras gathered around Zippy. Golly cleared his throat, "I'm sorry, Zippy. You are brave. In fact, you have the widest stripes of us all. Only your white stripes are so wide, your body can't hold them all."

Zippy smiled as he glanced at his reflection. He didn't flinch or blink. For the first time ever, he saw a ZEBRA!

A NOTE FROM DR. RICK METRICK

Zippy and the Stripes of Courage is creatively designed to open doors of communication with young children about facing, accepting, and overcoming physical deformities. Candida Sullivan's companion book, *Underneath the Scars*, is the story of her unique struggles and victories with Amniotic Band Syndrome.

Parents and therapists are encouraged to use Zippy's experiences as a springboard to help physically deformed children face, accept and overcome their individual struggles.

Discussion Suggestions:

- "Am I still a zebra if I don't have stripes?" allows for discussion concerning self-esteem, self-worth, and body image. (See Psalm 139:14)
- Zippy's tears offer an opportunity to normalize the existence and expression of sorrow, fear, grief, anger, etc.
- Feeling and facing fear is Zippy's badge of courage. Parents need to remind their children that courage can only happen in the presence of fear.
- Fear and discomfort felt by others is often masked by bullying and teasing. Zippy had to look beyond the teasing in order to feel empowered to socialize and avoid resentment.
- Zippy had many questions for God. Questioning God is not a sin. God is big, loving, and very understanding. Our questions don't frustrate Him and can actually be used to bring healing. (see 1 Peter 5:7)
- It is natural to want to hurt those who hurt us. It is supernatural to help those who hurt us. (see Matthew 5:10-12)
- Discuss with your children what it means to be brave. Help them understand the difference between vulnerability (the struggles of having a physical deformity) and resiliency (the ability to bounce back from the struggles). As them what they can do to overcome the struggles, themselves.

Dr. Rick Metrick has a PhD in Christian Counseling Psychology and is a Licensed Professional Counselor (LPC) and Approved Licensed Professional Supervisor (ALPS). He is the senior pastor of Jones Memorial Baptist Church and the Director of Total Life Counseling located in Beckley, West Virginia. Rick is also the founder of the Just Honor God movement (www.JustHonorGod.com), host of God's Wake-Up Call Podcast, and author of several books including *Just Honor God: The 27-Day Challenge*.

ABOUT THE AUTHOR

Candida Sullivan believes in miracles. She was born with a rare condition called Amniotic Band Syndrome, which generally causes death in most babies before they are ever born. She knows that it a beautiful blessing she survived and wants to show the world that her scars are not a punishment, but instead are a wonderful expression exemplifying God's love and mercy for her life. She believes God spared her for a reason and wants to spend her life telling of the hope and love God placed inside of her.

Candida lives in Tennessee with her husband Shannon and two boys, Cayden and Jordon. She teaches Sunday school and loves to be surrounded by the wonder and excitement of kids.

See Candida's book for adults, *Underneath the Scars*, for her story about how she overcame her struggles of dealing with Amniotic Band Syndrome.

ABOUT THE ILLUSTRATOR

Jack Foster was born in Chicago Illinois and attended the American Academy of Art in Chicago. After several years as political cartoonist for the Elgin Courier News, Jack knew that he wanted to take his God-given talent in a different direction. While teaching Sunday school in 2006, he made the decision to pursue children's book illustrating. God has blessed him with the opportunity to illustrate over a dozen books. He is married, with five children and ten grandchildren.

Note from Jack:
"After reading the manuscript for Zippy and the Stripes of Courage, I really wanted to illustrate it. God made each of us just the way He wanted. He doesn't make mistakes. I am so blessed to be the illustrator for Candida's wonderful story that reveals this truth to Zippy and to us, through his pain, his sadness, and his love."

ABOUT AMNIOTIC BAND SYNDROME

Amniotic Band Syndrome (ABS) is a rare condition caused by string-like bands in the amniotic sac. These bands can entangle the umbilical cord or other parts of the baby's body. The constriction can cause a variety of problems depending on where they are located and how tightly they are wrapped. The complications from ABS vary. Mild banding can result in amputation or scarring, while severe banding can result in death of the baby.

The medical community cannot truly explain what causes amniotic bands to form. While some call it a fluke of nature, I believe it is a symbol of God's amazing miracles. God doesn't punish us with scars; He blesses us with life. The scars show the world that there is a God and He is great.

AUTHOR'S ACKNOWLEDGEMENTS

I would like to thank God, foremost – the center of my life. My God exemplifies everything wonderful, beautiful, great, and loving in my life. He blessed me with the vision for this book. Thank you God, for being so wonderfully patient with me, as I fought and struggled against your plan for me. Thank you for helping me to find acceptance through Zippy and his many revisions. Thank you for blessing me to love and share him. And most of all, thank you for loving me and allowing me to live. Thank you God, for giving me scars to remind me of your great love and mercy just for me and my life.

I have learned that it takes many people to write and complete just one book. In my experience, there were many tears and prayers needed to complete *Zippy and the Stripes of Courage*. God blessed me with some amazingly strong people to help me along this journey. I would love to take a moment and thank them for their prayers, kindness, love, and support. Without them, none of this would be possible.

Thank you to ALL of my family and friends who encourage me, support me, believe in me, and love me. You will never know how much you mean to me! I decided not to list names on the premise that I might miss someone; however, I hope you know how grateful I am to have you in my life.

I feel so blessed to have worked with the wonderful people at ShadeTree Publishing. They exceeded my expectations on every level. Thank you for your kindness, this wonderful opportunity, and for believing in me. I could not have asked for a better publishing experience. You all are amazing!